Journey Inside

A Collection of Poems

by

Gwen Alford-Pean

African Heritage Press
San Francisco • Lagos
2003

San Francisco	Lagos
African Heritage Press P.O.Box 170613 San Francisco,CA 94117	23 Unity Road, Ikeja Lagos, Nigeria
Phone:415 4698676 E-mail afroheritage9760@aol.com URL:WWW.afroheritagepress.com	Phone: 234-1-4972044 080-33128151 E-mail: infoplan2000@yahoo.com

Copyright 2003 Gwen Alford

Library of congress catalog Number: 2002117435.

Cover Design: African Heritage Press

[Selections: 2003]

Journey Inside;
Poetry, Litereture, Cultural Studies, African Studies, African Literature, History.Philosohy

ISBN 0-9628864-8-3

Dedicated to my minister and mentor
Dr. Carol E. Dixon
& Her family:
Rick Dixon, Tasha Lewis, and Harley Dixon.

I appreciate your sacrifices and ever abiding love.

Contents

Introduction

"For all things are for your sake that the abundant grace might through the thanksgiving of many abound to the glory of God. For which cause we faint not; but though our outward *man* perish, yet the inward *man* is renewed day by day. For our light affliction, which is but for a moment, works for us a far more exceeding and eternal weight of glory. While we do not look at the things which are seen, but at the things which are not seen, for the things which are seen are temporary, but the things which are not seen are eternal."(2 Cor. 4:15-18)

Journey inside is a book of poems written as I traveled inside myself searching for truth. I lived outside myself placing my values on what others did and said about me. Inside, I found a place to hide and develop and deal with the outside from a new birth. I began by praying and reading my bible everyday and committed myself to the word of God and it changed my inner self. I discovered truth and it helped me find myself, God, and purpose. I could make decisions from the Spirit inside me and trust myself. I was no longer a stranger to God and my true existence. Everything began to make sense and come together and feel complete. The more I read about God and his plan for the world I felt more comfortable about my future. Being spiritual makes me feel fulfilled and not empty as before. I feel a part of everything and connected to everything and not isolated. It made me love nature and the other things around me and feel I am a part of the master plan. I also felt a responsibility for the word of God to be fulfilled in every area of my life.

I returned to college to continue my education but found a reality that truth can be used in many ways to change our world and how we live it. I redefined myself and found writing to be my joy and purpose. A lot of these poems were written after prayers

and meditations. It began with a simple assignment of writing a journal of feeling about things on a daily basis and to my surprise it came out as poetry. I realized it had been years since I wrote any poem, it had been since I was a very young girl. I had many who really inspired me to continue writing. My mother, Sammie Alford, my minister, Dr. Carol E. Dixon, my professors, Dr. Jane Schaberg, Dr. Latta, Dr. JoAnne Isbey, and Dr. Judy A. McCown, at University of Detroit Mercy. I wrote this book for myself, my children and my grandchildren to see the real me. They can look at pictures after I am gone but it takes words to express the true character inside. I share my truth that God is real and lives inside me. I found a joy for community work and a deeper love for my sisters and brothers. My writing will change as I change inside and I plan to build on truth to speak for those that are silent in my community. I am committed to writing and speaking the hurt and pain and the joys celebrated when all fail and the opportunity to feel what you say in your heart and tell it to all mankind.

Gwen Alford-Pean
Detroit, Michigan

Stepping Up

I can always feel when it's my time to step up to the plate.

    There is no time for me to hesitate.

I know I am to make a home run.

    That is the way the game is won.

The devil is pitching and trying to strike me out.

    I pick up the bat and give God some praise and a shout.

I've played him before and know his tricks

    He doesn't know I found out the game is already fixed.

God has my back and gives the calls.

    His promise to me is not to let me fall.

I am ready now and things are set.

    Devil this is one game you will never forget.

I just laugh at the devil while he really puts on a show

    trying to look professional as he goes.

What he does not know is, I know, the winner is not him or me.

    Our lives were given to give God the Glory.

My Best

I will give you the shirt off my back.
Will it keep you warm?
I will give you my last dime.
How long will it feed you?
I can love you and give you great joy,
Will you remember it tomorrow?
I want the best for you,
Will that make you want the best for yourself?
I can encourage you,
Can that give you faith to believe?
I can make you laugh and relieve your problems,
When I leave, the problem still remains.
I can give you advice,
Experiences teach you what I can not tell you.
I can smile and brighten your day,
I cannot turn on the light within you.
I wish all your dreams could come true.
I cannot give you the dream.
I can tell you of things to come.
I cannot change fate or destiny.
I can introduce the God within me,
to the God within you, and I've given you my best.

Maximum Potential

I can reach maximum potential
because someone has my back
Who loves and prays and never gives me any slack.
I spin my wheels round and round
Going fast but never leaving the ground.
The goals are easier reached
If I stop and listen as others teach.
These things I do not want to hear;
But are placed in my heart to hold very near.
Wisdom cannot be bought or sold.
It is the richness of life given to the rightful old.
Mom, this is the part, in which you play,
for you have prayed for me day after day.
I may not be all you wanted me to be.
 But, Mom, look inside and see a new me.

Homelessness

Into this country I was born
Not accepted by anyone.
Many fought for those like me
to enjoy others liberty.
Whatever liberty they set
Was all the liberty we could get.
How can I feel that I belong?
In a place I cannot call home?
The Italians are from Italy and
The Chinese are from China.
The Africans do not accept me,
All I know is I'm from my mommy.
Can you imagine how it feels?
Not to come from nowhere.
To live in a country
Where you do not belong
And do not fit anywhere.
My homelessness is deep within
and hard for me to express.
But I dream you will open your arms
and embrace my seed,
So this homelessness can die with me.

Not For Sale

I thank God for taking me off the block
for others to price and stalk me out.

My slave days were over long ago.
I am paid by the hour and not for what
I know.

I awaken to education just to have a
voice to speak
to tell the story of a hurting community.

I stand proud of being redefined, and
renewed,
With Christ Jesus, chief cornerstone, is
what it took.

No matter how free inside God make
me,
I wake up and see a dying community.

Hoping my life example of integrity can
heal destruction and despair,
it is the first thing I can do to start
somewhere.

But each and everyday I realize it is not
enough,
when I turn on the news and hear some
more stuff.

I am trying hard to work with my
family,
And encourage them to live a better way
as part of the community.

A new quality of living produced by a new character in God,
A kind of experience being spread abroad.

With God I celebrate the true victory,
And all I have to say is, "come eat and drink,
without price and money."

To God

I felt it hard to be in your grace.
I wanted to put a smile on your face.
I grew up thinking you were far, far, away.
And judging everything I do day after day.
Once I began reading your Word,
I understood you from the things you said.
It's hard to believe you love me so much,
until I'm in your presence and feel your love touch.
And the special signs you give to me.
God, I thank you, for your grace and mercy.
Amen.

God Seed

I am the seed planted in the heart of God.
My body, a living sacrifice, attached to His umbilical
cord.

I grow in Him because He is the way
No one can ever lead me astray.

As I increase He expands.
His will is always my command.

I am faithful in the Body of Christ,
working the harvest without strife.

Praying, touching, and loving my way through,
Just finding joy in everything I do.

I will work until the end of time.
Then I will be resurrected in his glory divine.

Deep Sea

At the bottom of the sea, a treasure is there
For us to know how much God cares.

He puts it in the deep for us to find
That His love was there all the time.

All we need is wrapped in his love
The things we need are from above.

His deeds are ecclesiastical
To humans this sometimes seem incomprehensible.

He is not like me, that is hard to understand
My thoughts try to make him a man.

But he is a spirit that comes as a bright light
Not to be compared to anything known in your life.

When He speaks, the anxiety, joy and peace I feel
Even though I cannot see him, I know He is real.

How real He is seems hard for me to explain
I know when I'm in His presence; my life is in His hand.

A hand that is strong and mighty but rocks me so gentle,
And speaks words of love and go right through me.

It is as if wind blows through my body full of holes.
And my mind, lost in ecstasy without a goal

Free from every thought I ever had before,
Freshness in His heart to last forever more.

Hit the Alarm

Hey, how is today going to be, good or bad?

Is it too early to tell? You look like hell. Please claim the victory!

Can I offer you words of encouragement to help you up and out?

Or did your mind say, stay in the bed and pout?

I think you ought to get up and get out because it is such a beautiful day.

But I am just your conscience what do I know anyway.

Do not go out into the world acting like a fool.

Looking and behaving crazy without a plan of what to do.

To spill your attitude and get a thrill,

On the one that says, "Hi, how are you, today".

The Thrill To Be

I am looking and searching everywhere,
for something new and exciting.

Something that has never happened to me,
I call it, **The Thrill to Be.**

It is that part of me I cannot touch,
The mystery of it is just too much.

I wake up wondering if today it will be,
that wonderful thing, **The Thrill to Be.**

It will blow my mind when it comes,
Take all of me as we become one.

What's on my mind, Look in my eyes and see,
All I can think about is **The Thrill to Be.**

I tried sex, drugs, games and fame,
but they left me feeling the same.

I know, nothing I have had is what I seek,
Nothing I can taste, touch, smell or see.

Guess What? To my surprise, I found **The Thrill to Be**,
It was buried deep inside me.

The Mix

I found this within me

The opportunity to reach for the stars and extend a hand to others

The fruit of the Spirit, love,

Joy, peace, longsuffering, temperance,

faith, goodness, gentleness, and meekness.

The King is anointing, A new quality of living produced by a new

character in God.

To love God with a perfect heart and willing soul.

To give all and know God is doing the giving.

To love and honor my Mother and Father in the highest Spirit of God.

Treasures from God that turns into rewards.

The enemy, inner me, is replaced by the Spirit of God.

i am Blessed

i am blessed because i walk not in the council of the ungodly,
 or sit in the way of sinners, nor sit in the seat of the scornful.
My transgression is forgiven and sin is covered.
 The Lord does not count against me,
 and in my spirit there is no deceit.
i am poor in spirit, and i have the kingdom of heaven.
i am comforted when i mourn.
i am meek and will inherit the earth.
i am filled because i am hungry and thirsty for righteousness.
i am merciful and obtain mercy.
i am pure in heart because i see God.
i am a peacemaker and called the child of God.

Little Living

If I feel everything that goes wrong only happens to me,

If I am always complaining,

If I see everyday the same,

If I cannot wish the best for friends,

If getting high is the only way to get by,

If the thrill on the hill is the only emotion I can feel,

If my success is measured by what others do,

If only what I think is important,

If I feel I could cash in my life for one problem, then I am living little.

I called upon the Lord in my distress and he placed me in a large place.

He increased my spirit and I can not live little anymore.

Getting Started

Trying to get pass Go.
Why am I not gone?
Where am I supposed to be?
What is stopping me?
Where is this force coming from?
STOP. PRAY!
Kill procrastination,
rebuke slothfulness,
evict confusion
and tell everyone else to get back
because I am coming through
and I will not stop until
I reach my destination for this day.
It shall be as God says it is.
Let there be!
Let there be!
Let there be!
And it was just that way.

My Seed Grows into Feminity

I redefined myself after a lifetime of oppression
    And not realizing I was oppressed, but a strong Black woman
Raising four children the best I can,
    with my family giving me a helping hand.
I thought Feminity was for white women, who lost their husbands,
    Or children growing up and going away.
That life was foreign to me and my family,
    And somehow I knew my issues were not on the table.
The man leaving was sometimes the best thing,
    After having to take care of him and all the misery he would bring.
Then as a feminist I read of Black Women strong in their way,
    But never being pampered, not a single day.
A tear began to flow down my face
    And I knew they had hit a very sensitive place.
I thought about my mother, her mother and all the women I knew,
    And deep in my heart I knew it was true.
I realized, that moment, it was time to fight for change,
    so I redefined myself and gave meaning to my name.
My name is Gwendolyn, strong, peaceful and loving,
    The things I grew up to become.
The truth within me was defined as three things;
    a child of God, universal being, and homelessness.

Just For You

I feel your sorrow and I feel your pain.
You feel your dreams have dried up like desert land.
What you need is the Word of God,
and let it fill your heart.
Nothing is simple and can easily be fixed.
But, prayer and the word is a mighty mix.
Your hope becomes faith by hearing the Word of God.
And you can make it against all odds.
There is nothing new to tell that you want to hear,
but God loves you and wants to take away all your fears.

A Perfect Day

I thank you God for those days I begin with prayer,
and you teach me how to be aware.
Of the things to be done,
as I see the rising of the sun.
I have blessed assurance, I am in His will,
because of the peace I feel.
I have favor with everyone I meet,
while goodness and mercy is following me.
Everywhere I go, there seem to be, no one shopping but me.
As soon as I get in line, a crowd of people is right behind.
Then I smile to myself because I know that is the way,
The anointing guided me through A Perfect Day.

My Friend

Jesus took the thorn
for me to take the scorn.
The bad mouth and hatred
I receive from day to day.
Jesus said this would surely be
If you suffer you will reign with Me.
What people say will not get me down
I choose to laugh and not frown.
I lift my head and will not fear
The Holy Spirit is always near.
Those forces seem to never end
but I find rest in Jesus, my Friend.

God At Home

Let me find my place in you
where I can forever rest.

So I can begin to show the world your very best.

Where I can just lay down and prop up my feet,
and feel freely to be what I want to be.

I will be so comfortable in you,
My presence will just glow through.

Many will recognize me when they feel my presence
and see your smile that will brighten up their day.

Others will just look at you and say,
"you're different in a weird kind of way."

But most of all I want you to feel
as comfortable with me as I am with you.

For when I am at home in you,
My kingdom is there, too.

My children All

My children were once my reason for dealing with things of life.
At each point I was stuck, they reminded me of Why.
My job was to do whatever it took for us to survive,
and not to count the times I had to swallow my pride.
Then there were times I would feel so very low,
their love was all I needed to get up and go.
Now I am older and the harvest of joy has come in,
we all get together and realize we can be friends.
My little ones have become big ones and a few grand's am I blessed,
to enjoy the love of family and put the work to rest.
I have learned to love them just the way they are.
And ask God to bless them with integrity of heart.

Running From My Shadow

It's just before daybreak, trying to find peace,
    Before my shadow wakes up with me.
How can I get rid of him?
    He haunts and nags me with that stupid grin.
I know what he's thinking but he doesn't know I know.
    He is just an ass that follows me where ever I go.
He thinks he's slick and he'd better not make me mad.
    If he does, I'll leave his ass right here in bed.
He stabs me in the back, calls me names, and say it's for play.
    He talks too much and never has anything good to say.
Criticize, murmur and complain each and everyday.
    I say to myself, "if I could get rid of him then I'll be O.K."
This monkey on my back thinks he's here to stay.
    I remember the words of my mother speaking to me.
"Honey, find the truth and let it make you free."
    So I found a cure for my disease.
When I got down on my rusty knees.
    I asked God to help me please.
Take this shadow that has me in defeat.
    I'm so low, I'm looking up at my feet.
God *please* have mercy on me
God said, "your shadow is a part of you.
    and what you ask I will not do."
But, rise and shine the light has come.
    It will put darkness on the run.
The effect of your shadow I will put in the past.
    Your soul is free at last,
and as the light increases.
    You will find that shadow under your feet.

September 11, 2001

How do I feel when I can't feel anything?
How can I cry when there is not a tear?
Yet, the sorrow and fear of today has struck my heart
Telling me disaster has happened.
How do I really feel?
I want to mourn but I don't know how.
All those lives taken have changed the course of my life now.
When the plane hit, it was like a movie or skit.
But, now I know it was real and have left me asking,
How do you feel?
It was like I've seen it a thousand times on TV
and it was just something to see.
The numbness in my body makes me feel like it has gone to sleep.
My soul cries out from defeat
"Tell me it didn't happen"
I want to go back to today, just an ordinary day, no cares coming my way.
Remembering when I woke this morning with nothing on my mind.
Got up and went to work at the same time.
Looking out the window and just chewing some gum.
My supervisor says, "Come and watch TV a crisis has come"
Looking at the second plane as it hit the building.
Wondering what kind of picture is he watching.
Then, he said, "This is not a movie, this is real."
I sat down in my chair wondering,
How do I feel?

The Temple

You fuss about the dust, but welcome the lust.
Honey, keep The Temple clean.

You're green with envy and gossip with the enemy.
Honey, keep The Temple clean.

You lost your cool and felt like a fool.
Honey, keep The Temple clean.

You feel sorry for yourself and mad at everyone else.
Honey, keep The Temple clean.

You tell a little lie and then wonder why.
Honey, keep The Temple clean.

You don't want to obey but just have your way.
Honey, keep The Temple clean.

You cannot give anyone anything but free advice.
Honey, keep The Temple clean.

Your words if swallowed be bitter in the stomach.
Honey, keep The Temple clean.

You will not forgive because you want revenge,
Honey, keep The Temple clean.

For if you keep The Temple clean.

EVERYONE EVERYWHERE, will be SOMEBODY.

True Confessions

Can God come without his glory?
   Can we believe half the story?
      Should we listen to what others say?
        And not read our Bible everyday?

Some say I believe in God
   But I only call him for the big job
      The little things I can do myself
         He can take off and go help someone else
            There are some things I like doing alone
               I don't need him to wash, cook, or answer the phone.

           Will we walk in holiness and give God our all?
          Or do we need a little more time to wait upon our call?
       Many say give me time, what I'm doing is not a crime.
That holiness stuff is not for me but I will work with the prosperity.
Everyone is not the same and God knows and understands.
Did he look into our eyes when he said, "Let us make man?"

Joy

For years sex was my feel good and I had to have it to be happy
But the Word of God began to clean and make me holy
I knew it was against God and my body
But I did not know how to make myself free
I just knew there was something for me to do about my sin
Not knowing that prayer and the Word would bring it to an end
I fought with my weakness for many years
Sometimes losing hope and crying many tears
Saying some days that this is just how life is
Some things we can change but others we have to deal with
while continuing our wrongs without feeling any guilt.
It took years of praying and reading the Word of God
before I received victory from the flesh of sexual lust.
I received Joy boiling inside of me
Like a vulcano erupting of good feelings indeed
I could have all I wanted, exceedingly
And nothing attached and no one to please
I could not believe I could just wake up and feel so good
No matter what I do or what I go through
I could have Joy and no one could ever take it from me.
It was a blessing from God and I will never let it go, no matter what.
I WILL HAVE MY JOY.

Please Answer Me

If I don't love
How do I know it exists?

If I'm not kind
Can there be kindness?

If I do not give
Will anyone receive?

If I don't pray
Can change come to me?

If I don't find truth
Will only my soul be lost?

Can I find the answer if I never ask the question?

Becoming an Activist

Who can speak for me out of the silence of my heart?
When I am living like an animal using the power to survive.
I know now why all my rights have passed me by.
I have yet to be defined as human in my mind.
I was given the ability to make rational decisions,
not only for me but my community.
So I decided to become an activist to speak for those in need,
to say what is silent in their hearts but cannot be spoken in peace.
The fight is to keep the power to survive that is challenged everyday.
How can you fight for the rights of people who fee
if you leave me alone I can live?
Survival had become a violent fight that makes us kill each other.
I have the love to put a thousand to flight.
If one joins me we can put ten thousand to flight.
Where Is the Love?

Tree Of Life

I see a tree of multi-cultural society,
sharing one history.
All lives, building with one goal in mind,
to have a future of all kinds.
Sharing our difference with love and pride,
but, knowing you are by my side.
Not always to mix and measure but mutual respect
The power of the mind has made us all great in a special kind of way;
to bring energies together, building a new wave and a new day.
Let's begin a history that includes us all and the things we do
big or small,
called, the Human Race.

The Light

No longer darkness
                  my sufferings became light
       lead me
          to things
a path   to win
        new beginnings
            take fear away
I was   I am no more
    New meaning   different course
      Listen   say to me

      what I feel internally.
The order of orders I must obey
As I receive them distinctly day after day.
To direct my destiny as I go about
Spreading the light from the inside out.

The Heart Of A Black Woman

MY HEART IS BIGGER THAN YOU AND ME,
IT CARRIES IN IT THE IDEAS TO BE.
A WORLD OF GOOD TASTE AND PLENTY OF COLOR,
THAT WILL EMBRACE MY SISTERS AND MY BROTHERS.
my pursuance is always to balance the scales,
no matter what trepidation I receive from hell.
My pounding becomes my rhythm of life,
It makes music and stays free from strife.
All of my pain has become pure joy,
not because I am happy but because of what I know.
I don't want my life to end up in vain,
And leave this life just the way I began.
I feel it is not about trying to change everything,
To really be equal to a man might make me lose more that gain.
My goal of success isn't against man, but to influence and be
included in his plan.
I tried to take the man out of the woman
and the he out of her,
but I realized there were not enough left of me.
So to find my own, can not be done alone,
so please, will you please, help me just find my identity.
I want to feel the decision you make all the time,
are made with me on your mind.
WHEN I WAS YOUNG, I HAD PLENTY OF LOVE,
AND SOME TO SPARE.
YOU COULD FIND MY LOVE ALMOST ANYWHERE.

IT WAS A NATURAL RESOURCE
OF WHICH I HAD PLENTY,
AND I ALWAYS MET THE MAN WHO DID'T HAVE ANY.
I GAVE IT ALL WITH NO REGRET.
KNOWING HE COULD NEVER GIVE IT BACK.
That part of me became like open space,
it started to ache and feel lonely.
Then a message came from my mind to me saying,
"That love you gave was not from thee."
IT WAS FROM GOD DIVINE
AND YOU SHALL REGAIN IT;
IT'S JUST A MATTER OF TIME.
Now I send my love to the earth and galaxies afar,
To fall like dew on mankind wherever they are.
So as they start out their today,
I can help life to move in a more positive way.
Now I beat to the rhythm of the Boss.
Afraid if I stop, then I will be lost.
the tears are all behind me,
though they never got me anywhere but misery and pain
and to find out that no one really cared.
I guess it must have filled the ocean or maybe helped the rain,
and sometimes it did relieve the pain.
I found out a broken heart will make life just stand,
and not able to move unless it has a helping hand.
YES I AM THE HEART OF A BLACK WOMAN

MADE STRONG! STRONG! STRONG!
TO GO ON, AND ON, AND ON.

God I thank you, for the heart you've given me,

And I hope in return, I can be the best human being possible.

Printed in the United Kingdom
by Lightning Source UK Ltd.
107300UKS00001B/171